In the Park of Culture

In the Park of Culture

Edward Falco

University of Notre Dame Press

Notre Dame, Indiana

Published by the University of Notre Dame Press
Notre Dame, Indiana 46556
www.undpress.nd.edu
All Rights Reserved

Manufactured in the United States of America

Library of Congress Cataloging-in-Publication Data

Falco, Edward.
    In the park of culture / Edward Falco.
        p.   cm.
    ISBN 0-268-02875-3 (acid-free paper)
    ISBN 0-268-02876-1 (pbk. : acid-free paper)
    I. Title.
    PS3556.A367I5   2005
    813'.54—dc22

                                    2005001137

∞ *This book was printed on acid free paper.*

For my brother, Frank Falco,
who brought music and art home

and for Steve and Clorinda Gibson,
with thanks for a lifetime of sustaining friendship

Contents

The Passion Flower

Acknowledgments

The short fictions in *In the Park of Culture* have been published as follows:

Akros Review: "St. Augustine on MONY Tower"
Aspen Journal of the Arts: "Memories"
Black Warrior Review: "There at the Circle" and "At Fifty"
BluePenny Quarterly: "Summer Flowers" and "Out Here"
Carolina Quarterly: "Night Drives"
Confrontation: "Picture from a War Zone"
Exquisite Corpse: "Communion"
Greenfield Review: "Bodies"
Hiram Poetry Review: "In the Green Drawing Room at Hollins College"
Indiana Review: "Leningrad 1942" and "St. Francis Protecting This World"
Iowa Review: "Brooklyn" and "Magic"
Mid-American Review: "Delivery" and "A Child before St. Jerome"
Montana Review: "Rowing Home"
New River: "Night Water Night"
New Virginia Review: "Winter Light"
Notre Dame Review: "The Body of a Woman" and "Essay on the Eve of War"
Pennsylvania Review: "Winners"
Pequod: "Harsh Thunder"
Quarterly West: "Five Women in a Bed"
St. Andrews Review: "Summer Light"
Sou'wester: "Marietta Goretti at Nettuno," and "Ursula at Cologne"
Southern Humanities Review: "The Passion Flower"

Smoke Signals: "Saints at the End of the World"
Spoon River Poetry Review: "Winter Lake"
Sundog: The Southeast Review: "On Memorial Court"
Telescope: "A Dealer in Antiquities Remembers . . ." and
   "Jumping the Fence"
Western Humanities Review: "Pen and Ink / Watercolor" and
   "Casting Out"
West Hills Review: "Voyage"
Xavier Review: "Concert in the Park of Culture"

"Bodies," "Blizzard," "Jumping the Fence," and "Voyage" were reprinted in *Montana Review* 8 (*Time Enough for the World*).

The following are collected in *Concert in the Park of Culture,* a limited edition chapbook from Tamarack Editions: "Concert in the Park of Culture," "Delivery," "Harsh Thunder," "Jumping the Fence," "Ursula at Cologne," "A Dealer in Antiquities Remembers . . . ," and "Picture from a War Zone."

"St. Augustine on MONY Tower" is collected in *Plato at Scratch Daniel's and Other Stories,* University of Arkansas Press.

Hypertext versions of "Five Women in a Bed" and "Summer Flowers" are collected in *Sea Island,* published in *The Eastgate Quarterly Review of Hypertext* 2.1.

In the Park of Culture

Jumping the Fence

The right moment, the moment of release, is a matter of faith. He slides from the swing pumped to a smooth half-circle as ten-foot lengths of chain at the peak of their arc come close to collapse, his body as precise as time. When he slides from that seat he must be right: too late he clears the fence and rolls across glass-seeded concrete, too soon he'll never hold. He's eleven and seems unaware: only "jumping the fence," though somewhere in his eyes a small white coffin must sail beneath Christ's cross, his mother the way she rocked and wailed and seemed at times lost in a place hidden in her body. The way his brother walked: trailed, a little shadow, behind the older boys. At six he jumped the fence in the corner park. At seven he missed, came down in a maze of metal bars designed for play, broke apart, two days later died. I wonder now, as he pushes that swing to its limit, where he'll find the strength to let go, what saint will whisper in his ear.

In Naples last year, at the Church of St. Peter Martyr, Vincent Ferrer bent over a dismembered child. Through the artist Colantonio's eyes the arms, legs, and head severed from torso: the child then restored by Christ's power; by St. Vincent returned to wholeness he prays at the feet of father and mother. And in Champaign, Illinois, a woman returned from the dead. On a metal table laid out in a morgue the detective in charge at her side the body turned warmer, skin found color. "I'm telling you," the detective said, "I saw a resurrection." Though for the doctors it was only something they could name, hypothermia; her revival rare but no mystery. The detective remained convinced. As did scores of observers who, on the 5th of April in 1198, saw Christina of Stolmmeln fly up to the church rafters; or the best intellects of their time watching St. Thomas Aquinas levitate as he prayed. Or in Western Springs, Alabama: on the six o'clock news television cameras file through a long corridor with hundreds of faithful to see the face of Christ patterned in the wood grain of a hospital door: the father of an injured child prayed for a sign. A story I didn't follow, I don't know what happened.

But that seven-year-old boy, whose brother now hesitates on a swing that sounds like screaming, remains dead. As do all the dead I've ever known. My father's father, who grasped my hand as he shut his eyes for the last time. My sister, just fifteen, at the hands of a man who was seen but never found. I think of that man having heard such men may lead normal lives, and wonder if he lives securely somewhere, with perhaps a wife and child, having put that darkness from his past out of mind. Or if he worries for his soul. They found her two years later in a remote upstate park—a set of bones wearing a red sweater, pants still securely fastened pulled down below the hips. Shoes and bra scattered nearby. I think of her there unfound through the changing seasons: her flesh wastes, an animal claws at her side, becoming a child's bad dream, a skeleton dressed in tatters, a grinning skull above a bright red sweater. I think of that man praying, and the boy I'm watching lets the swing's gathered momentum subside. When it is still he dismounts and walks away slowly, his hands pushed deep in his pockets, his head bowed to the ground.

4

A Child before St. Jerome

You are impressive in a New York museum, bracketed by two of Rembrandt's most famous portraits. This is El Greco's vision, "St. Jerome as Cardinal," though you were never a cardinal: refused even the habit of a cleric unless it came without obligation. Recluse, hermit, whose mass was offered under burning sun in a desert so hot "it frightens even the monks that inhabit it." There you suffered the body's willfulness: in a scalding cave visions of Roman women danced and you groveled, licked sand, struck yourself to be rid of them.

But here you have passed through such suffering. Your eyes heavy with age and the world's order hold a child transfixed. He looks grave beyond his six or seven years as he looks up into your eyes and his own eyes shine with awe and wonder. At the sight of a long white beard falling from cheeks like dark holes. At eyes like caves, and a body so frail and emaciated hidden within a cardinal's bold red habit. He knows nothing about the fever of your youth, the love for things worldly and voluptuous, the passion for Cicero and brilliant pagans: Jerome of the world before Death uncovered a spindly arm, snatched away closest companions and brushed your cheek with a scorched black knuckle. You took to God then and I imagine your eyes in the desert not unlike the eyes of this child stunned by the figure of a man alight with authority and anguish.

How different from the sufferer with a dark opening in his chest where he beats himself with a stone, with a hand deformed, skin that sucks at his bones, who flees something unseen behind him, his eyes blinded teeth broken hair shorn, tortured against a background of stone. Which is da Vinci's "The Penitent Jerome." Which comes to mind and floats above the child whose wonder has turned to worry as he takes a step backward and scampers for his father, not knowing, I'm sure, what it is that frightens him, but feeling it there in the pit of his heart: the quick stinging rush of blood that follows instantly the recognition of danger.

Ursula at Cologne

You would never guess women were being massacred on Memling's canvas. The colors are so lovely. Seen through the gold frame of Byzantine arches, under a blue sky, the white marble spires of Cologne majestic in the background, Ursula appears calm as she holds up her hand to deny a suitor; he, the palm of his hand facing hers, as if about to touch, is serene, perhaps resolved.

She is about to die. The purple folds of her gown lie gently on the ground. In a moment her executioner will release the arrow readied to pierce her heart and she will crumple to sainthood. But not in the moment Memling has chosen. Here a small white dog, companion to martyrs, sits peacefully at its master's feet, delicate paws lazily crossed, eyes turned casually upward. Here you must look carefully to find the carnage.

The soldier at Ursula's side, dressed handsomely in a quilted white tunic, has impaled a woman on his spear, though it's difficult to notice, separated as he is from his victim by the framing column. Following the line of his spear, you notice a girl with a sword through her breast. Blood rushes toward her hands pressed together in prayer. She is falling into the arms of a woman already fallen. And beside them, a child with an arrow through her arm. Then the soldiers: an archer taking aim, two carrying spears, another with a club raised about to strike one of Ursula's virgins. According to legend, ten thousand were murdered that day in Cologne. All Christian children following Ursula in holy pilgrimage.

Now in modern Cologne a church stands at the site of the murders, marked and remembered by an inscription on a stone, still legible so many centuries after. And, Memling's painting, "The Martyrdom of Ursula and her Maidens," much coveted, often displayed, reproduced by art books in total and in detail, where the slaughter is represented in colors that subdue, and attract, and command the appreciation of the viewer.

Marietta Goretti at Nettuno

Woman is the origin of all sin
and it is through her that we die.
        —Ecclesiasticus 25:24

Canonized in 1950. St. Maria Goretti, Victim of Holy Purity, whose remains are preserved at Nettuno, Italy.

Dead at twelve, in 1902, murdered.

Popes visit her now, in her shrine, where she has lain on her back stiff as a fallen mannequin for eighty years. She has not aged a jot who wears a white satin dress and holds in her right hand a slender white lily. She reminds, even now, of girls in line on their way to the altar. They wear white flowers in their hair, genuflect and bow as they step into the aisle. They cross themselves one at a time and take their places. In the corners of the church, at the backs of the aisles, nuns in black habits oversee their communion as gathered family watch.

The girls are careful in new dresses. Some pray to St. Agnes, patron saint and protectress: throat slashed in Rome, sixth century A.D. Others to St. Maria Goretti. They picture her as pictured in schoolbooks: red lips, pink cheeks, uplifted eyes surrounded by halo, soft cloud, blue sky. So different from her pale rigid corpse at Nettuno. And both different still from the child at the top of the stairs mending clothes for her mother, where she sat when her attacker entered. A local boy, several years her elder, who stabbed her repeatedly when she would not surrender. Sentenced to thirty years in prison, he served twenty-seven, was alive at her canonization.

And: St. Agatha, breasts torn off for refusing a consul's advances. St. Julitta, sawn in half by Spaniards. St. Catherine, finally beheaded. They are many.

As Marietta, virgin and martyr, forever dead in her narrow shrine: a child becoming a girl becoming woman.

Voyage

This is a tower like the one he climbed at Notre Dame. The rooms at each landing impossible. There should be nothing beyond each arched opening in stone but damp night air; instead, rooms with brightly colored tapestries hanging from the walls. Rooms that, though empty, suggest activity. Each tempts him to delay the long climb to a part of the tower where. . . . It doesn't occur to him to wonder. Bent over, he carries a heavy burden of something on his back, toiling in good spirit up the narrow spire where the weight of unknown others has worn smooth crescents in the center of each step, turned stone to air.

At one landing his father sits on the edge of a bed, taking off his shoes. It doesn't bother him then to see his father, dead several years, smile and gesture as if pleased at the encounter.

He says, 'I have a family now. My girls are almost grown."

His father smiles but does not answer.

He continues up the stairs.

Takes a moment to rest in Cap-Chat, Canada, on a rocky beach looking out over the St. Lawrence River. Shifts the weight on his back.

"This is lovely country," he says. His father's youngest brother kneels beside him, wife and three children watching from farther up the beach. They are on the Gaspe Peninsula, at the end of the Notre Dame Mountains, where he and his wife often vacation. "I was sorry," he says, "to hear of your accident."

His uncle nods.

He looks at his aunt and is shocked by her appearance. She looks young and sad, like a sullen adolescent. He turns to comment, sees his uncle too is young, much younger than he is.

He shakes his head.

His uncle stands and walks away.

He watches the whole family wade out into the water.

At his feet a starfish, which his wife believes a sign of good luck. He stares for a moment at its death-stiffened, lifeless arms, and when he bends to pick it up he hears them behind him.

And hurries up the tower not knowing where he is going, but desperate to keep a circle of stairs between him and the others: his father, his friends, those he has loved who now march behind him.

Pen and Ink/Watercolor

—after a drawing by my brother

Someone's face behind a watch, framed by the circle of the watch, is at the center of it all: this picture you've drawn which tells a story. The eyes at three and nine o'clock are staring at the viewer, not angry but unrelenting, as if demanding an answer to an unspoken question. A crooked line ticks seconds across his forehead. His lips are shut tight. He is not speaking. Apparently it is the job of the seer to decipher the story. Or is it a riddle?

The man beneath the watch is our father, dead how many years still all the time in our dreams. Last night or the night before, he was sick again, his head grown round, his hair fallen out. You were there when two strangers lifted him from the couch, lowered him into a black plastic bag, pulled the zipper closed. Which illustrates our differences. You stayed to supervise, watched him placed in the back of a station wagon, carted away like abandoned merchandise, like something unwanted. In the kitchen with the women, I said I preferred not to see but was afraid as I was afraid of so many things those days.

In your drawing he is healthy, leaning back in a chair, uncharacteristically pensive, his eyes fixed on nothing. Above him, chin starting at his crown, is the bottom half of a face. It dominates the right side of the picture and needs no explaining: No one's face in particular, it is, teeth gnashing grinding, the face of someone dying, a woman beaten, a survivor looking at the body of a loved one. If it had eyes it could see,

13

running in a line through the center of this scene, indecipherable calligraphy that suggests or signifies writing.

That's me under the scrawl running out of the picture. Or was me the years drifting from person to person, place to place, before the comfort the pleasure of belonging. You portray me as a runner, the disembodied hands of a clock floating over my shoulders, pointing at my back. Above me, proportionally massive as a building, a typewriter holds a blank sheet of paper. The allusion to writing is easy. The ridged surface of the watch's crown seems to mesh with the knob of the typewriter's platen, as if they were gears: the winding down of the watch turns the platen, loss of time a catalyst to creation.

And above the typewriter, the profile of a pirate which you contend you cannot see.

Regardless, this is what I see in your drawing. That's you inside the watch. Your story says we are surrounded by pain and death and marked by time. Why else the pirate Death peering over blank paper, dressed in headband and eye patch? Why else am I running pursued by time?

If it's a riddle you've sent, I cannot answer. If a story, I've read it, and yes I understand.

A Dealer in Antiquities Remembers . . .

He had dark hair, Freud, and a handsome gray beard. I first met him in 1925 in Vienna. My father had a shop next to a small café. We dealt in antiquities: it was the kind of shop customers browsed through for hours before making a selection. Years later it was destroyed when Hitler came to power. Don't ask of the running. Only I of all my family survived and I prefer not to remember. Then, I was twenty and Vienna was lovely.

The doctor had an office at Bergasse 19. I went around for my father who was already too old for the walk and the stairs. Sometimes as often as twice a week I'd shuffle through his door carrying alabaster urns and primitive pieces. His room was a museum, his desk cluttered with shapes carved and sculpted: animals and demons, exotic men and women. I remember an African god, half man half bird, chiseled in stone; a porcelain figure of an Indian girl asleep on the back of a bull. These things he valued, strange knickknacks to others. He sometimes, I was told, stared for hours at one of our figures. They gave him inspiration, started him following an idea.

With Freud my father never haggled. We were both awed and, I think, a little frightened. My father remembered him much younger—when his face was fuller, his eyes more lively. When I knew him he was dying of cancer. He covered his mouth, which I guessed was disfigured. "Make it fast," he told me. "I'm in pain. I don't want to talk."

Once, I was bringing him a piece I was sure would make him happy. Twenty years earlier my father sold him something just as odd; and Freud, as father told it, danced around the room. It was a carving of a man, a woman, and a creature with the genitals of a woman, and the torso and face of a man—all writhing in the palm of a proportionally massive hand. But when I placed it on his desk he only stared for a moment and then turned away.

It took him, I have heard, a long time to die. The last thing I sold him was the arm of an Egyptian mummy clutching an ankh in its gauzy fist.

This he bought holding a rag over most of his face, his eyes dark and humorless, full of something between anger and fear.

Blizzard

—March 12, 1888

At first I tried to follow the sidewalks. I have an apartment on the East Side of Manhattan, five blocks from work, and when I got outside snow and ice flew down between buildings and turned me around. Then I was surprised. Later I read winds gusted to eighty miles an hour and the temperature dropped to minus eleven; but that Monday it was just cold and snowy, and I was on my way to the office.

After two blocks I huddled close to a stone building hoping for warmth and pulled my scarf tighter to my face. It was a battle just to keep moving. Then a gust hit me and I rolled like falling down a steep hill and when the wind turned me loose I was lost in a city I had known a lifetime.

The street was slick with ice. I stood where I knew I must be surrounded by familiar buildings and I stared and squinted, but all I could see was a gray cloud of snow. When I tried to move I fell, and I knocked my head against the icy street. Then I slipped again and I rolled till I came up against something solid, and when I braced myself against it to get my balance I saw it was a man the snow had covered. I looked for a long moment into his blue, bruised face, frozen as hard as meat in a freezer. Then I was afraid—though, still, I could hardly believe the danger.

This time when I stood I turned my back to the wind and I let it push me sliding over ice till I wound up pressed against the red brick of a

17

building, and I hugged that wall like another life as I made my way slowly through the blizzard. I came, finally, to two wooden doors with windows, and when I let myself in that hallway, I knew where I was— on the corner of my own block, three houses from where I started. For a long time I looked at my reflection in the windows. My face was swollen and covered with scrapes and bruises, and there was a gash above my eye that ran all the way to the hairline. It spread wide and deep, but it wasn't bleeding, and when I looked harder I saw my hair and most of my forehead were covered with a clear, icy sleet. Mrs. Polumpus came out of her apartment and screamed when she saw me. Her husband and son helped me to their sofa and covered me with blankets.

I was out in that blizzard for less than an hour. I was in the hospital recovering for more than a week. Even now when I walk these five short blocks to work I remember that man I stumbled over. I picture him as he got up that morning in his Manhattan apartment; as he looked out the window and grumbled about snow; as, dressed warmly, he closed his apartment door behind him and started for his job in the heart of a crowded city on a workday morning.

Harsh Thunder

Over drumlins thunder lasts, rolls through time: black sky a thick skin shaken. The highway is numbered but the number doesn't matter. Only the storm he walks into, and the moments before the storm when air starts to crack and hum.

What was is behind him: years that never happened. He dreamed the starry skin of women, legs and thighs like lightning, muscled as fast cars, and found children, and a job that went from nine to five, and dusty weekends, and nights asleep in his clothes on furnishings that owned him.

So this highway that leads to other highways that cross the country claims him, and he leaves tracking New York mud through Pennsylvania, West Virginia, Kentucky, heads south and west for warmer weather, dreams again of where the road will take him, of bodies that open for him, of meals served in a home that mounts a hillside, cars, planes. As does: The Mexican walking toward him two thousand miles distant. The Vietnamese colonel who boards a foreign plane. A black kid, waits under the Atlantic City boardwalk. A white man, turns away from a Georgia farm.

Evening approaches and they all grow hungry.

The sky flies out over all of them, and holds them together in its dreamless weather.

Picture from a War Zone

He stands above the others, hands at his sides. Under the circle of his face there is nothing, so skin falls slack and expressionless. Under his eyes an abyss the balls sink into drawing weak flesh down. This is the face of a man who has lost his children. It is a face not unlike the five dead children laid out before him. They are spread in a neat semi-circle beneath the outstretched arms of their kneeling mother. Her eyes are closed and she laughs through her teeth. Her children stare at her with vacant faces: behind their closed eyes nothing happens, not even the constant night-dreams of bombs like drumbeats and fiery soldiers. Above them the sky is as blank as the depths of the ocean, as empty as their father's eyes.

St. Francis Protecting This World

The saint's body, a sail spread over the planet. Christ with speared lightning clasped in upraised arm: around this god angels cower and Mary, Earthly mother, grasps her bared, human breast that fed him, begs Christ's mercy for the world. This is Reubens'"St. Francis of Assisi Protecting the World from the Wrath of Christ," Musee des Beaux Arts, Brussels. Outside, on cobblestone streets, a thin rain: August 8, 1983, and young Belgians, faces painted death masks, lie down in traffic. This day thirty-eight years ago the bombing of Nagasaki. One girl holds a picture of a man whose face is burned featureless by the flash.

Later this month, 1883, Krakatoa, an island the size of Manhattan, is destroyed. Many are burned and the sky fills so thick with ash they are left without light. They bump into the fallen as someone on a distant ship sees a mushroom cloud of mud and pumice spread over the island and is awed by the wonders of nature. This is the planet St. Francis protects, his right hand over the Pacific Ocean, where waves flew inland that day, dropped ships and bodies on hilltops. Thirty-five thousand died and what survives the eruption offends the eye: a derelict gray mound above water.

Beyond St. Francis's cape cities burn, sacked by foreign armies, a woman about to be raped is pulled down by her hair. The saint looks up from this snake-encircled globe he loves beyond reason, fearful for his planet. Here, where god threatens man with such fire, holds cramped in his heart such violence, even the best of men looks to the sky wounded and disbelieving.

Moving

1

This dog lying forlornly at my feet, sad I won't walk the woods again, won't take him with me to bound up hills, leap fallen trees as if in flight, weave at speed knowing every twig and leaf, we named Puck when a puppy, after a spirit in Shakespeare's play, and the name fit like prophecy: grown, he's still into everything. He lies at my feet frowning, looking wistfully from my eyes to the woods.

In the kitchen behind us, where he tore a cloth calendar off the wall, Anne leans against the sink drinking champagne with her sister, celebrating the closing. I can see them behind me through a bay window that looks out on mountains, where Puck looks up from time to time and whines at the sight of Jill toddling through the kitchen.

Last night we walked these woods together. Under a full moon Puck found thoroughfares and ran ahead while I walked warily. In a clearing I stopped and remembered a night when the dead lay heaped in their village, the ground discolored by blood, and afterward watching the sunrise as I walked back to base tired and numb; and when Puck leapt into the clearing I noticed at the foot of a tree a broken mirror. It caught the moon in its pieces. It caught my reflection as I stood above it and I saw myself divided, looking down at a firmament in pieces. Behind me Puck pointed his muzzle at the stars and the moon drew out its song.

Later that night, in bed with Anne and Jill, I woke to the sound of Puck snarling and looked down from the bedroom window to see the woods alive with whispers and rustling: Puck at ready, his teeth bared for a low, dangerous growl. I waited till whatever it was passed and Puck curled up again in moonlight; then I lay a long while awake and uneasy.

2

Puck's in the cellar. Sitting in a chair beside my daughter's bed, I think ahead to mornings she'll lay her head upon the red sweater Anne wears through winter nights. Beyond them, through the kitchen window, mountains and trees dressed in new snow, and at the counter Anne sleepy, auburn hair unkempt fallen over her shoulders, Jill in blue pajamas, half asleep on her mother's shoulder. The three of us together, as much each other as ourselves, among morning light and color.

Leningrad 1942

There's an image from the siege of Leningrad I can't forget.

When the fall of the city seemed near, children were put on boats and sent across Lake Ladoga to escape the Germans. The people of Leningrad watched from the shore as German shells sank those boats.

They watched the silent white caps of their children floating on the lake's dark water.

Concert in the Park of Culture

—Vinnitsa, 1939

Under fruit trees Ukrainians dance. Spring breaks hearts; music wracks the cold harmony of nature.

Underfoot, deep underfoot, absent loves molder. Bullet wounds worm peasants, farmers, soldiers: exiles who never left home.

At the Sunday concert in the Park of Culture daughters eat fruit sweetened by fathers and brothers; wives dance on their husbands' bones.

Bodies

Someplace in England a workman summoned to clean a sewer finds the drain clogged with human arms. The flesh is black or rotted, laid out in a dark skin of wet leaf and slime. Slick. Deceptive. The workman wonders at what he sees: gnarled fingers scorched, indignant, point to something without them, in all directions, as if to say (once he knows what he sees) Be careful. Look there. Someone's coming.

He backs up slowly, though he won't find safety.

In New York when the East River thaws or at least turns warmer bodies pop to the surface nudged out of muddy hiding by restless gases. Every spring the expanding bodies, so a police launch patrols the river, gaffs the dark bales that burden the water's surface and hauls them in. The attempts made at identification are most often useless. No one knows where they come from, but they come every spring. While men on the launch drink beer and try to make this assignment pleasant, yell out something when they spot a floater.

Or in Chicago, when Gacy boasted of the killings and kept men digging for months. Or on a migrant-worked farm in Los Angeles. Or the Chattahoochee River. Or Katyn Forest. Or what's under the Park of Culture in the Russian Ukraine. Or . . . Take your choice: anywhere a body settles.

As on the plains outside Leander, Texas: a road crew beginning work on a highway uncovers a body where it's lain ten thousand years. And still she looks sleepy, curled up in her shallow grave. Her bones almost make a circle, like a child cuddled head to knees. She too floats to the surface, a gentle reminder we didn't need. They name her Leanderthal Woman and dig deeper, in case there are others. They leave nothing uncovered, take it all to a museum, house her in a special display circled by worthless trinkets they've polished to glitter. As if out of a desire to increase our wonder at what lies everywhere beneath us—how deep, how far back.

On Memorial Court

Eight limestone pylons sail forty feet skyward, frame the polished grain of a dark marble cenotaph: massive cube, centered, immovably heavy. It's spring. Early morning sunlight, no cloud, Memorial Court overlooks the Virginia Tech drill field, a girl in red jacket, white pants, crossing the green oval. My back to the mall, I turn forty looking over the campus where I've worked ten years, and trying still to course an old sea of memory.

All around, carved on the inner face of pylons, names of men who, like the girl now climbing the steps of Williams Hall, attended classes here, crossed the drill field on a spring morning when the sun was bright and the air full of calling, as it is now, this morning when the world is empty of their children. My father's talk of Normandy, of a brother dead where ocean still washes with salt water the open wounds of men, all I know of the second world war. I try to imagine that uncle alive among our computers and VCRs, and I have no trouble at all, till I hear myself whisper, "Nothing changes but the size of the killing," and I'm surprised by a fist that closes in my throat, the way I begin to breathe hard.

Spring, fifteen years ago: half a million fighting in rice paddies, jungles; 50,000, 60,000 in Washington, D.C. Troops line the roof of the Justice Department. We're shouting *Peace*. Then the muffled *pop* of a gas canister. Then others, and screams and pushing: a girl faints as gas scrapes the soft jell of eyes, lungs, frightens. When it's over we drive two hundred miles. Someone in the back of the van plays an expensive guitar. Some of us talk, still excited or angry. Some sleep. We drive through the night.

In a narrow kitchen, in Brooklyn, an uncle who survived the slaughter at Corregidor spits on the floor at my feet and leaves the room. Father

28

leaves with him, mother follows. I stay away a long time. On the sub-
way in Boston, beg for nickels and dimes. Sleep with strangers, vagrant,
spend time in jail. Take drugs that pull me under: months, months walk
with fear, the night's scorched landscape. Messages in trees, in the way a
blade of grass moves, in the words of strangers. Till I'm so surrounded
by fear, even buried in the body of a willing lover still at heart alone.

Then, on a beach in California, I wake in bed with a child, a girl thir-
teen, fourteen years old, and stare hard a long time hoping something
will change: the dirt in her hair thick and matted to her pillow, the black
mascara clumped to her eyelids, the ugly smell of sweat and cigarettes.
It's cold in the sunlight that lights up the room. Sweat circles the small
of her back. I shiver as I see us walking the beach at night: the eye of a
creature winks among scudding clouds, the ocean laughs like a woman
grieving, tears off its clothes and throws them again and again on shore.
She put her hand in my back pocket. I could barely see her, the way
everything shifts and shatters. Sea gulls flock somewhere on a dark
beach. I want to be carried high in a white beak and dropped to rocks
where this hard shell sealed with the salt and grime of fear will break
open. A window broke. The gritty sand suspended in the sweat of our
bodies cut us open.

That was the farthest I traveled, that was what I found. I left my clothes
beside her, left her asleep in sunlight, stole a set of clothes that fit,
climbed out quietly the broken window, hitchhiked East and home to
find years had passed. Six months later, back in school, hair cut neatly
just above the ears, the war in Vietnam falling toward its end, as all
things return to what they were, till now, somehow, I'm forty, married,
two children, own a house with a mortgage, worry about interest rates
and merit raises, and surprised to be so moved by the names of the dead
on a war memorial.

Inside me there's something that gave up on reaching light. It was
buried in the debris that covered Vietnam. It closed its eyes and turned
and has refused to look again at a girl running naked from her burning
village, boys from Kansas cutting ears off corpses, dangling men from
helicopters, since brushed by war's burned hand. Fifteen years and still
nothing's the same, no one untouched. Not this beautiful campus surrounded by mountains, where students walk hand in hand through ivy
tunnels, some among them in training for the next war, and within me
something still hides its head, preferring darkness.

Whatever it is, it's not dead. It turns in the cramped space where it lives. It feels sometimes when looking over mountains, quiet before furrowed green hills, like a hawk or a kettle of hawks traveling a long tunnel, flying hard for light; or—looking out over the drill field now, as class time approaches and the circle fills with young men and young women—like arms of light trembling at my side.

Vincent was my uncle's name, the one who died in France, and since there's comfort in imagining, I see him jogging on his way to class. I see him wrestling with a limber wife. And since there's nothing here to calm the rest, other names on other tombs, I step down, join the circle's bright procession, and leave them buried where they are, in ground and heart, doing the damage they deserve.

Saints at the End of the World

Last night I dreamed of the end of the world: nations floated in the sea, separated from continents. They drifted calmly. People waited on city stoops, knowing nothing was coming.

I watched a child cross the street with St. John of the Cross: we were all saints, but no one was rejoicing. We were starving. Flesh fell away from our bones. Little remained but spirit. Still, there was no rejoicing. There was only starvation and death and the end of the world, and our spirits sank and we heard a mournful voice whisper, "the soul is not immortal and death ends all," and we cried through the night till the low moan of wind over the river woke me.

Essay On the Eve of War

—October 2002

Her desire to touch while mouths bellow this and that about war, about killing. The need to, in this season of random shooting, of bomb and poison. She's sick of the posturing, of the attitudes of righteousness, after which so many wind up dead. And that's part of the desire to touch and be touched without the hand then closing like a fist and yanking her into the bloody feast, the civilized hall. Leave us out, but do come here because out there it's blood weather again. Come here and let's make a place where we know each other by what's in our hearts, where we worship and nurture with sheltering bodies, reaching through skin to the place where it's not just one person anymore but all the teeming others ageless, multitudinous, beautiful in various skins that in this place we know to be one body so that our touch touches everything that breathes and is alive. And then, maybe after that, we can go out to-gether and tell stories of a different world, a place where we know the loved one in others and act accordingly, where swords in the hands of warriors are playthings, toys with which they gesture like bellicose chil-dren or harmless fools.

There at the Circle

Rowing Home

The water's surface so mirrored sky and tall weeds along the channel's bank, it didn't require imagination to see down as up or up as down, mid-afternoon, alone, rowing a dark green boat under a blue summer sky. From time to time I'd stop to listen, sounds water makes even in silence: carp roughing its way through weeds, bass or pike or another carp breaking water.

Those channels formed a maze off Lake Ontario and I'd quit being careful, as once in mid-winter I went out for a walk in the wind of a snowstorm. It was a night that comes when you've lived a long time alone: when snow blew, I walked through thick fog, found myself outside the city and kept walking still. The road dirt frozen, slick ponds of ice, on either side field-stubble, and somewhere I guessed a fence, though I couldn't see it. Wind whispered in my ear, I walked blind, and that night I might have walked for nothing had the road not led to someone's house and white light from inside cut a hole to crawl out of darkness. Before I knocked on the door and told them I was lost, and they gave me hot coffee and a towel to dry my hair and hung my coat over the oven while one fished in the cold cellar for someone's old hat; before they drove me home, the old couple, to my two-room apartment in the city, I watched through the dining room window, the old man in his overstuffed chair, feet up on an ottoman, and others with him: his wife, with a pattern spread on the floor; her daughter-in-law kneeling alongside her, busy with scissors; and the son lying on the couch half-asleep—asleep on his chest, her feet dangling over his thighs, her head snug under his chin, their daughter, June, with the grandmother's blue eyes, the mother's dark hair. I watched for the longest time, till wind stopped talking, and I felt cold bitterly.

Drifting that great quiet, oars stowed in the boat, I came up on solid land, and a tree with branches that overhung the water, its wide trunk close to a boulder, and I heard them speaking, though they hadn't seen me, the girl in a flaming pink dress, color surprising everything around, the boy in a clean pair of blue jeans and a western shirt, red and sequined. They stood barefoot atop the boulder, ten feet above water, grasping a yellow nylon rope tied to the tree's farthest branch, and while I watched she screamed and he yelled and tree and rope swung two bathers in a perfect arc over the channel, and together they let go, and together they disappeared under water, and when their fiery bodies came up out of blue water, they came up laughing, and nothing remained the same and alone, not wind or water or someone watching—and I took out the oars, and started, again, rowing home.

At Fifty

Sometimes at night there was nothing to do but get on my bike and let black streets rip past, my heart wild for something there was nothing of and I knew it watching the night slice by between the streetlights till the streetlights were gone and I was out on mountain roads heading for rocks that overlooked the valley. Not some rebel standing on a cliff, a kid with the wind in his hair and in the back of his mind the dramatic figure he cut as if he were someone's hero. I was fifty. I was there because the rough weather in my heart never let go. It rocked me god all my life rising up at times like something furious and it was still there not even the roar of the engine or standing on a precipice over the valley with wind blowing through my clothes could quiet that thunder out of nowhere the same lightning from youth only then I knew there was only one kind of roar or another in answer and nothing would ever quiet it nothing ever and nothing was meant to and it was not romantic or dramatic at all except maybe the sense sometimes that came of all the others all the others ages and ages.

Passion's

red seed healthy in the stomach's soil its web of roots. Father, his fist is night descending, hurtling down, the impact deepest in the body. The impact deepest in the body. The way it learns its own inadequacies shame fear I took these with me for a lifetime, my father's lessons. Every slap the shock absorbed in tissue reverberates. A clock chimed in the body's tunnels.

The moral choice made with doubt at war through words action inaction weapons in the ways we destroy and create, attentive or inattentive. Then dream the moment everything changed. These rise up nights asleep, touch something hidden the shape that moves along the ground out of sight rippling through leaves against a fallen branch. Opening, changing.

The way the dark overwhelmed as a child. Something behind, under the bed, in the closet. Mother mother turning her hand her hand inflicting pain, her sharp voice his hands what you saw his body her body stepped out of the bath, the foreign body that lives beneath familiar clothes.

Deep in the stomach the red seed its web of roots grows. What can you tell me, I tell you? Love is a part of it: the sun's last rays flaming through trees, a loved body against lips and tongue. And knowledge, the world's body shifting and changing, the solid we learn is not solid, the stars we see that we know aren't there, assumptions that fall away like the dead generation by generation.

All unsayable, not-words: a web beside which a spider's work is gross and clumsy. Mother, father, husband, wife, lover, the ordinary the cordial smile, a lie. What we are: a long scream a howl a sheet of flame unfurling. The red seed's web of roots spreads along the cheek in the moments when restraint fails. Speak out of order words like fingers feeling toward grass blasted jukebox shock of music speed the child a hand of spirit mist condensing light a long line of red light stretching from the open heart of out of the open heart of into the, open

Night Water Night

Black dock.
Slice of water at night.
Moving river water.
A woman in a red coat, looking off at—
A girl, really.
She's at the end of the dock.
If she spoke her voice would be blown away by the breeze.

———

So you are about to enter into the sexual flow and movement that will be your life, as if stepping into a river. You are in body a girl a young woman standing on the edge of a dock at night and I don't know don't have any way of knowing what it is you're really thinking you are really doing out there at night a girl in a red coat at the edge of the dock looking out over the river.

You never saw that I was there looking at you though I was only a few feet away.

I lay on my side half asleep on the bridge of a friend's boat.

You appeared in the early hours of the morning I checked my wristwatch when I first saw you walk out of darkness surrounded by night breezes and bells clanging from a few boats rocking water it was a little after three in the morning and I was shocked when I saw how young you were a teenager alone on a dock at night you stood at the edge of the dock in a red jacket and looked out over water.

In the moonlight I could see your face I could see your eyes I was a shadow on a boat looking at a girl on a dock looking out with such sadness at moving water.

———

Out of your sadness.
Depths watery dark.
Sound moves slowly.
The weight of your sadness a force.
Your eyes move over the river as if water were your sister.
Your eyes the river at night.
What is it that is feminine about this sadness?
Muffled.
Dark.
Embraced.

———

A woman once pulled me to her body. We were in the hallway of her house, there was no one else around. She took my arms by the wrists and pressed my hands hard against her breasts. You want me, she said. I know you want me. Then she pushed me away and went angrily to her bedroom where she slammed the door.

This happened in a time of drama in a time of confusion. She was married. Her husband was my friend.

I am a man now nearing sixty years old.

That moment, the river flowing fast.

She was right. I did want her. For a time, I loved her.

This was many years ago and she is long since dead. Her husband is remarried with a new family and I can still remember the feel of her youth under my hands the electric resilience of her body we were like a flame up there in the bedroom hallway I still don't know if I behaved as a decent man or a coward.

I want to reach across the darkness and embrace you not with lust but with gratitude.

A girl entering into the body and life of a woman.

––––––

Air moves and the night's music moves through air.
The breeze touches her face like a father who loves his daughter.

––––––

Your nearness is loss.
I am something else now.
I am a father I am a husband.
The sight of you is loss.
The air around your body warmed by skin.
Knowing I am outside the circle of young women is loss.
The air around you breathes, it shares your life.
The night river which you think is other flows for you.
You are a force as elemental as the binding powers.
A young woman in a red jacket looking out over water and night.

––––––

I arrived at her door in a loud city. It was her parents' house and they
were gone, at work. We were both in our twenties. She came to the
door wrapped in a towel. A thick red terrycloth towel knotted over her
breasts. Her legs and neck and face still moist from the shower. Her hair
wet, slicked back. I can't remember for sure what we did. I think we
made love. But the moment when she opened the door, the silent house
beyond her, one hand holding a red towel at her breasts, invitation in
her eyes, wet hair and moist skin. . . . That moment is as alive as this
one, when the moist night air blows over the river while a young
woman looks out into the night.

––––––

Love's dive to cat's strut, sail to God.
Enter into air, dissolution of body.
Nowhere, nowhere, even your skin disappears.

––––––

Either this world is the world or this world is not the world and no one knows. No one knows either this world or the world that is not the world. Either this mask is this skin is the world or it's not. No one knows. And so how do we live? Either we live for this moment in this world or we don't. If this world is a mask and there is another world then how do we live? Is it a task? Is it one movement in a larger composition? Either this world is the world or there is a power like light and love humming under our skin that is something more than this world than us. This is what you live with, this question. When you extend your hand so that the tips of your fingers touch the skin of a man's face are you the hand of God are you a piece of light becoming the movement of light through time are you a piece of God doing God's bidding are you becoming God in the reach of your hand making that connection—or are you an animal doing what animals do? Or are they the same thing? When you die will your body rot and become the body of the world which in time will rot and in time return to the nothing from which we all spring as animals as this world? Or will you go on? There are many who believe we go on. When you touch a man's face these questions are the movement of your fingers on his skin.

———

    The child emerges.
    The single self is pulled and in a moment destroyed.
    Out of you.
    Into you.

———

You walk away and leave me and the dock empty.

There is still the sound of water there is still the clanging of bells and warmth that comes with absence.

It's as if the years are moving water.

I have sailed along the current of years to this place where you are embarking.

Old man looking at a young woman in the quiet of river and night.

The Body of a Woman

What is it about some men and the body of a woman? For some men, a woman's body is like the deep sound whales make under water, a sweet urgent calling from another place, almost impossible to resist. Like Odysseus they must strap themselves to a mast and suffer to refuse the song of a woman's body.

What is it that makes his breath suddenly go shallow when a woman, undressed, bent at the waist, dries her dark hair with a green towel? Her breasts are small, nipples tucked in within enfolding skin. Why does he need to touch those breasts—with the palm of his hand, with his fingertips, with his mouth, the mouth most urgently?

It's not the animal urge to procreate. Not just that. Not for some men. For some men just to look is enough, just to see the body of a woman: the way the lower back dips along the spine, then rises to the parted flesh of the buttocks and falls again to that star of light where the legs meet the body, that small empty space, a diamond of nothing but desire.

This is not about love. This is not about a union of spirit that goes higher or deeper than the body. This is about the body itself, the body of a woman: the nape of the neck; the slope of a leg; the opening into her, the way flesh mounds there. Just to see it for some men is a reckless urge.

Does it have something to do with death or beauty? Is it only the instinct to survive?

In my dream the body of a woman was a luminous door, a glowing plane in a dark field, a passage, an entrance, a way into a hidden place I was meant to find.

What is it about the body of a woman? What is it about, the body?

Summer Flowers

River coiled sunlight aluminum boat, she wore shorts and a loose white blouse. I was twenty-three, she was twenty. I had just returned and she was married.

This flower opens bright petals drifting the river opens around us on an island where we stopped to gather flowers. She bent to water and threw scooped handfuls, her legs tan feet up to the ankles in blue-green water. Behind her a smooth slope of hard-packed sand rises to the island. She's bent over the water, her hands coming up a child's mischievous smile, her eyes are blue her hair blond, her breasts free under the white blouse. Water glistens as it crosses a short distance through air to a place where I am moving toward her across water. She is walking backward to the island, to a green meadow thick with wildflowers.

Then there was an affair that lasted a few weeks a month and then some ugliness between me and my friend who was also her husband. I can barely remember, forty years between then and now.

But the way she bent to the water, the way her breasts moved under a loose white blouse, the tan of her legs emerging from the blue-green of water and the way water glistened flying out of her scooped hands, the island behind her, the flower opening around us. We were the center we were whatever it is that blooms we were that opening as she stepped back to the meadow in the heat of a summer morning and that moment after forty years its warmth like sun, a face turned to sunlight, the sun on water warming across the moment we never choose when we are the center, a meadow untended.

Five Women in a Bed

Five women at a party jump on their host's bed. Women, not the idea of women. Someone takes a picture. After that flash preserves two red blouses, a blue skirt, shoes, curve of leg, curve of thigh.

———

He stood by the door watching.

———

I'm standing by the door, behind the woman behind the camera, below and to the right looking on. To see me, you must expand the picture.

———

I'm alone at the party, he was alone at the party: outside the picture.

———

A lifeboat floats on rough water. There are five women in the boat. In the foreground, a man is swimming, only the back of his head and shoulders visible. He is swimming hard toward the lifeboat.

———

Once I.

———

He stood by the door and watched the women as they clowned on the bed. They were all friends and he wanted to crawl into their arms and be comforted. He wanted them to destroy loss and death and bring him into their circle.

———

Life. Boat. Swimmer.

———

He was standing by the door watching and we all felt something we talked about it later. You could see it in his eyes. As if the bed were food and he were starving. It made us uncomfortable, and we.

———

He was alone at the party and a man and a woman coupled make a circle. The muscles of his back and chest, the give of breast and thigh, heat that builds to coolness. The last time you made love, right at the moment of climax, where were you where was your lover?

———

He was alone at the party, outside the picture. You could tell he was looking for a way in a way out. You could see it in his eyes. He wanted to crawl into bed with them he wanted to walk away from them. He wished there were someone who could answer who could ask.

———

This guy had this look like this look in his eyes like, this look.

Night Drives

At three A.M. I leaned against white tiles in my narrow box of a shower and let hot water stream hard on my stomach easing night cramps while you were someplace else for years by then, miles from all the promises from places so deep the air as we spoke like air before a storm that almost hum that skin-slight vibration.

Light off white tiles, I'm lit up bright as a movie screen. Outside dark quiet rural homes crickets' nightsong. When the pain won't stop I get in my car and drive past dorms where now even students have called it a night, past neat rows of houses, out onto gravel roads that fall through woods. I turn up the music, turn off the lights.

That went on for a year, waking like that, under the surface urgent, it scrabbling up a slick wall acrid acrid opening onto. Word scraps going bad and bubbling up the throat grit black. He did this she did that. He said. She said her words his words stored in cells twist in sleep words become pictures that tell the truth lying if need be: that's not her body you're shoveling dirt over or him mutilated on the side of the road, just a stranger you're crying near when you wake as if something's alive inside your body, something deep and just under the skin.

In the Green Drawing Room at Hollins College

Inside the Green Drawing Room there are two mirrors. The one at the front is oval and slightly concave; the one at the rear, a rectangle. Both are several feet high and wide, their gilded frames ornately carved. Between these mirrors, at a polished wood lectern facing rows of folding chairs, invited poets read.

Far from the Green Drawing Room, Virginia, or Hollins, I learned a love for poems. On the slate sidewalks of Brooklyn at eight or nine, a boy whose father taught him fear, I walked with my head down and my hands in my pockets, where once a high school kid pinned me against the concrete of a stoop and with a single punch broke my jaw, left me scraping my forehead against the rough sidewalk as he went his way grinning and cocky, having taught me once again how some of this world is a dumb animal mean in heart and dim mind.

In the Green Drawing Room at Hollins, I watch readers speak suspended calmly between images echoing wall to wall, sound and sight warm as a comforting dream, as a place where the baseball bat opens no one's head and the woman who lives upstairs doesn't sell her daughter by the night. It's someplace better than that; and, in the moment dizzied by word and image, just as real.

Sea Island

Spanish moss on live oaks, time fatigued by heat. Everything here slow, sand, salt air. Pasty white flesh washes away like a light layer of scum and a deep earthy brown shines out of the body. Hearts slow to waves and tide. At night electric storms slide along the ocean, eruptions of power and light, rips in the merge of water and sky on a night horizon.

Insects gorged on our ankles as I sat on the rocks with a friend. In front of us, the storm light. Behind us, our families asleep in a rented house. In the ocean that morning, in the roiling water, uniqueness and beauty fell away. The sea boiled. I rose up out of a tidal pool into sunlight, a consciousness that understood nothing. Breaking waves threatened.

One night we came upon an alligator in the surf. It looked to me like a log or a break in the sand. We were walking with our children, our two daughters and his son, and since we knew there were no alligators in the ocean, we approached it casually, until it turned and lifted itself up on its front legs.

Later that week, past midnight, we saw a deer on the beach, head bowed to black water; and at dawn, a dying woman carried on a stretcher by friends lifts her head weakly and turns her withered body to let her feet drop in the surf.

An alligator in the surf, a deer, a dying woman. My friend and I on the rocks watching a storm over the ocean. Our breaking, rushing in, drawn back out, night, stars, planets. What's in here, out there, rending, wrought, night and dawn sea life on a storm-drowned tree cast up in lightning, light, one time.

Casting Out

A pair of bees yellow jackets buzzing around a cow, a teenage boy in jeans and a T-shirt. Milk, glass shards, the hum of fields when down from barn rafters bees swarm and the boy swinging his arms the milk bucket spills, the coke bottle at his feet shatters under the cow's hoof and I'm on my back in the center of a barn milk straw grit in syrupy coke yellow jacket buzz and everything casting spun away the real world entering: glass shard, cracked seep of light through dark sting bright scream of heat as lurch walls lurch and the barn, the barn walls disappear like light changed as it travels through water into darkness a man a woman a child anyone lying under deep water on the floor in a barn and nothing is the same, the solid wall not solid as light waves its magician's hand points to the torn way under where milk and glass shards the roar of knowing the emptiness we are the down bees milk and blood pain of a lover's touch the mouth of a loved one compelled to bite until blood seeps out of another's body and onto dark lips in a darkened room where two bodies rock together or a single body at her desk, in his fenced-in yard, in the center of a gravel country road at three in the morning our arms all outstretched toward what we don't know we need ripped away and cast.

Possessions

A bass leaps out of water, disappears, is yours forever, just as that boy on tenement steps drugged and half drunk who wears aloneness like a thick black coat is yours, though twenty years distant. This is more than memory. This is the thing itself lets you in: what's outside, what's inside: the bass out of water, the self without love. These you own at the back of your heart, waiting that you come to them again.

Out Here

Out here in the dark, this dirt road cratered by weather, crossed six times by shallow creeks, trees and foliage on two sides, the town where we live its concrete and tar defined by street lights miles away.

In the air, mist. Above us, a semicircle of trees frail as a pencil sketch. Two in the morning where a popular tune plays all around, the sound of shallow water over rocks in a creek, song of this world, lyrics winding through and deep in the body.

We have been here before in this place like a last and first home and it has held us tight with no pain and no question.

———

Out here it can be cold and no light.

———

Dirt roadbed, water over rocks.

———

When I touch you you flare up for just part of a second like a great light. Then you recede to shadow. Then finally you go dark.

———

When I touch you it's like embracing a city whose inhabitants panic and run. Then stop and close their eyes, finding calm in that dark.

———

I'll leave you alone.

———

What's under our eyes is a shelled city, body after body and all of them our own. Here's *touch* mangled under rocks. Here's the time he did that next to the cold body of that other time in the basement.

———

And here we are together in this dark. We talk about the Gulf War and later we drive away separated by a buffer of silence, the people of our cities still in the rubble where they've come to feel at home.

———

Goodnight we say, when what we mean is *good-bye*.

Our envoys have returned to their hovels.

Magic

The circle we turned around the house disappearing piece by circle around we turned your news coming in a circle around you the news we turned around the house the words coming one by turning an incantation making the house disappear piece by grass baked in sun barefoot the lawnmower abandoned bright red machine piece of a deer's skull mingled bones brought back by Sage from hunting the nearby woods a piece of red ribbon blown from another yard piece by piece the house unravels disappears our life in that circle the news coming slowly to hurt less at last spinning out the circle the news till yes at last the news and we stop walking and I laugh because there's nothing else and you walk away from me and then back and I put the circle of my arms around you and you walk away chanting something you pick up the ribbon take it with you to the car drive away nodding and I one last turn of the circle nothing changed gone remains.

Winter Lake

On shore mosquitoes too thick to hide from. In woods beyond the camp's clearing, heavy rustling. I paddle my canoe onto Winter Lake, tie up securely to a tree stuck solid, huddle under thwarts wrapped in blankets—moon a bright circle, cold water moving under a thin metal hide.

When I close my eyes darkness settles in the palms of my hands. Night curls up where you used to lay your head and breathe as softly as now the night wind breathes.

Summer Light

Every night for days I dream how you left us: at four or five I open my eyes, you're away two years. That summer light that baked the grass as we circled our old house and words one after the other dismantled yard and garden—that summer light is two years gone.

In the dark I remind myself how flesh burned from your body on the way to that decision, and it makes it easier to close my eyes, my life changed still, the one of us, the plural I, falling away fast and silent, the two of us following paths that meet where a child holds us together.

When I wake it's morning. I stand by the window, look out at a field where we'd walk evenings, sunset to dark, and the memory warms as this morning sunlight warms, sunlight that burns fog off water-blue thistle, heats slate tiles on the roof where you live. The palm of my hand on glass touches your cheek: sleeping quietly in a quiet house, or walking at dawn with another.

Winter Light

Almost no light this morning: deep blue horizon, red brick house, trees winter pale. An icy wind swirls snowflakes I can count, so few whipped into a brown field; and nearby black hills, black lightless hills lined with white light, as if a child white-crayoned ridges, as if light seeped out from behind or inside.

I hurry out of the cold, warm my hands at the woodstove where spring three years ago when you lived here too a sparrow struggled in the black metal flue and we let it into our home to fly through our rooms leaving smudges on walls.

That was three years before this winter morning, a morning I make coffee for someone else thinking how I overheard a friend call me love's fool; and when a woman's voice calls me back to our old room, I go to her thinking the black hills are like whatever it is that rose up between us, sodden, heavy, soaking up light.

Memories

Four from Boyhood

one

Of a man's body tanned dark brown, smooth and hairless back and shoulders and waist, the skin turning white abruptly at the waist. The crease of his buttocks begins and is quickly hidden by the white cotton sheets at the edge of mother's bed, where the man sits hunched over, his feet on the floor, his right hand squeezing the back of his neck, his left hand holding his knee. Mother lies on her back, covered to the neck with sheets. The back of her right arm rests upon her forehead. Her hand is open, palm exposed. Her left hand holds the sheets to her neck. In the crook of her left arm her breast pushes against fabric.

Alongside her side of the bed, maybe a foot taller than the bed itself, I'm standing. The surrounding walls are white. There is no sound. There is an open door behind, and straight ahead sun shines through two windows, and, reflected by a hardwood floor, fills the room with light.

two

Hanging from the fence at the McCarren Park pool: a Cyclone fence, two of the crossed wire prongs at the top deep in my wrist. It is nighttime. A policeman stands below me. His head reaches my waist. He is pointing to a sign which reads *Admission 50¢*. Blood trickles from my wrist and adheres to the fence, coating the wire diamonds. Above, a full moon is shining. Behind, the dark rustle of trees after nightfall in a city. All around, the sound of voices young and old. Beyond the policeman I can see the underwater lights of the pool. Beneath the blue water the lights are the color of the moonlight. They move as the surface of the water moves: they form circles and oblongs, they split and come together, they ripple and sway, in constant motion beneath the blue water.

three

Seeing the city from a window on the sixtieth floor. In a waiting room with a rectangular opening cut into one wall where a secretary makes appointments and calls names. The room is lined with blue chairs. A half dozen people are waiting. I'm looking out the window behind a blue chair at the numberless buildings, at the traffic on the streets, at people huddled on corners, at bridges congested with cars and trucks, and I'm trying to comprehend the individuality of people. I'm telling myself that they all have friends, that they all have homes, that each of them has someone who loves him as my mother loves me, as I love my mother, that there are many cities in the world, some of them bigger than Manhattan, and all are full of people like me, like my mother.

four

Of a man standing at the top of the stairs, his face yellowish in the shabby light of the hallway; his face round, moon-like, stretched like a balloon. A mustache curves around his upper lip and down to his chin. He is dressed in boxer shorts and a sleeveless undershirt. His arms and shoulders are big. With his right hand he grips the banister, with his left hand he points down the stairs.

I am framed in the door to our apartment. Behind me my mother is approaching. Above me the man is shouting "whore! slut! bitch!" At the foot of the stairs on our landing, twenty feet away, a girl in a red dress is kneeling on her hands and knees. She is bleeding from her mouth and nose: blood falls from her face and splashes to the floor. Her hair is wet. It is knotted in long strands and still dripping water. Her red dress is wet, bunched at the waist and unbuttoned in the front. I can see her breasts and the slick white flesh of her thighs. There is a desperate look in her eyes. She is saying "please," but she is saying it softly, so softly I can barely hear.

One from My First Marriage

My wife's body a soft creamy white in moonlight through bedroom windows. Stretched out across the bed, her legs over my legs. My body is much darker, so much darker her skin flares where it crosses my skin. Together our bodies form a V, our legs meeting at the vertex. We lie on our backs. The palm of my hand touches the palm of her hand. It is summer. We are covered with a sheen of perspiration. Through the open windows a breeze carries the sounds of the city at night.

One, Recent, from My House in the Suburbs

Sitting in the recliner in the spare room with the portable television turned on low. Through the open door I am looking into our bedroom at the other end of the corridor. My wife is asleep with my daughter in her arms. The bedroom is neat and attractive: the brass headboard shines, the mahogany dresser gleams. My wife is beautiful. Her brown hair covers her neck and shoulders. Her face is turned toward me and looks slightly troubled, as though she were having a bad dream. My daughter is snuggled against her stomach, her arms wrapped around her mother's waist. It is late. It is after four in the morning. There is an old movie on the screen and all the house lights are turned up bright.

DeWolf Point

In Fellini's *Casanova,* Casanova on a river in Spain or Italy or France pulls at the oars of a wooden boat just as I pull at the oars of this aluminum boat here in the Thousand Islands on the St. Lawrence River. But it's not an imagined comparison between myself and Casanova that reminds me of the movie. It's the way the river looks. Fellini used long sheets of black plastic to represent water: it rippled and cracked and swelled in what I suppose was an artificial wind. This morning real wind rushes across the water, distressing the gray surface with white water, foam where the waves break open, and under this cloudy sky at dawn the way the dull morning light is absorbed by water, the way wind blows and water snaps reminds me of Casanova's search for romance on that black plastic river.

Yesterday Sunday in bright sunlight on still water my wife and I drifted along this same shoreline. We were fishing for bass and watching what went on in the backyards of the riverfront houses. Most spectacular was a man drowning a raccoon. He had it trapped in a wire cage weighted with rocks and it hissed like a cat as he lowered it at the end of a rope off his dock into the water. I saw the expression on his face turn to a grimace as the animal's fury turned to panic and the cage must have rocked under the water. Next door a man raked leaves. A few houses down a couple with a child ate breakfast on a porch overlooking the water.

An hour later I caught a good-sized bass which my wife cooked for dinner. I cleaned and gutted it, though that's a job I've never liked: there's something in the way the eyes dart and the skin quivers long after the head has been severed. But I did it, as I've always done it, as another man drowns a destructive raccoon, as another rakes leaves.

Today we've been married fifteen years. The children are home with her parents and we're taking a rare weekend alone. When she wakes she'll wonder where I've gone and guess I woke early and went fishing. She'll put on breakfast, bacon and eggs, once she's checked and found the boat missing. She expects me to return soon, as I am returning, pulling hard against the morning current, feeling tension in my arms my back my legs, sweat thickening on my forehead the wind lifting the water and rushing beneath it releasing for an instant a disturbing sound like the hiss of a half-starved beast or the breathing of an animal moments after capture when its skin still bristles with anger.

Brooklyn

Street buried in it buried street talisman glass Coke bottle bits of metal summer tar sticks buried in it buried metal bright silver dull copper glass bottles glass buried in it

Stoop concrete uneven stones rise up above the plane jump stoops rise up above the plane metal buried in jump buried stoops a face in the window buried in the street stoop window

Stickball the kids skinny broomstick pink rubber buried in it the ball streets sticky tar metal buried in it bits and pieces tar windows someone's face in the stoop window streets Cyclone fence pinned against it cars horns bikes

Lampposts brown rising up over the windows stoops streets fences back-yard brown paint flaking spin around spun legs around shinned lamppost stoop to window window even with the top of the stoop into a living room mom in there dad in there sister brother aunt uncle fence stoop window street buried under it in bits of bright metal plastic sometimes money buried under under it even now now after all these all this

Communion

Streets riot smoke boys rope dangles hands tip glows red smoke stoops second-story window. Fourth of July, 1959. Brooklyn. Streets full of smoke. The retarded kid stood on the corner pissing at passers-by. I told you the kids called me Rabbit and you said you knew what it meant. Liar. You carried lies in your heart like a black light. A steam of anger rose up out of you. Father of black fists.

July Fourth smoke filled the streets like fog the explosions cracks and glass breaking the whines roars rumble of thunder. His big brother stood outside our neighbor's front door. He howled out of rage tears wet in his eyes. The retarded kid's big brother. He lived on the corner. His mother owned the corner store. He stood on the street smoke coiling around him crying screaming at the neighbor's closed door.

I knew what this was all about. You took me into the bathroom. Yellow light. Shower tiles. You closed the door. You sat beside me. You put your hand on my knee and asked and the sounds leaked out: my throat rusty plumbing the words black water thick with sediment and filth.

Stoops

Not smooth surfaced ones like brownstones in better neighborhoods, but blond and rough-textured, with stones embedded. I could run my finger over a stone, the surface smooth, but only an instant before the ripping texture of concrete, ragged and sharp. Crisp angles perfect for the pink Spaldene to bounce back, high edge shot like a home run, kids cheering run! run! run! Or wooden stoops like bunk beds we'd lie down on when we were tired. Kids. Brooklyn. We'd jump off, climbing one step higher each time, until from the top step you could feel it in your spine. It might make the back of your head hurt. Where were our parents? I can't remember a parent ever to say stop. We jumped handrails to slate or concrete sidewalk on dares. We catapulted cast-iron spear-picket fences. We shinned up lampposts and hung off the top over traffic. Summers we ran the streets morning to dark, climbing barbed wire, crossing alleys, crawling through any opening. Only at night the mothers' voices like solitary birdcalls, your name singing along the darkening streets.

Winners

When the roulette wheel stops spinning and the ball turns descending in circles into exactly the slot that bears your number and the measuring gaze of the players falls on you at last at least for the briefest moment recognizing you you who started out with so many others from the wrong neighborhoods altogether brawling outside the doors of the casino happy at last just to be in the hall even bloody with spectators along the floor pushing toward players and when through lies and cunning and deceit and duplicity and passion and longing and desire and fear and single-minded will and hard labor you made your place at the wheel and dropped all you had piece by piece on the table winning a little losing more but holding your place until at last the ball turned descending around the polished wooden bowl into exactly the slot that bore exactly the right number and the players clapped politely and the croupier pushed your winnings to you and then finally it was over the pile of chips as large as you ever dreamed and somehow you were still young though hurt and not the same dressed in tailored clothes driving a bright red car down a mile-long driveway saying here I am, here I am, here I am, here I am, here I am: here, I, am.

Delivery

Pulled from deep-water stillness he came into the world through layers of muscle and blood. He looked about the room. His mother frightened on a table beneath him, stretched out, shaking, grievously wounded where he emerged. Others tended to her calmly in the brilliant white room: where light first pierced the darkness inside her, people hurried, anxious hands accosted every part of his body.

Her belly collapsed with his absence. Her body shuddered for its loss. His father—seated, holding his mother's hand—wore a face he had never worn before. The way it sometimes happens, alone or together: perhaps coupled mischievously in a roadside wood and at the right moment trees leaves elements respond *we are of you*, and everything changes. As lightning reveals itself to a solitary walker, charging a field with its secret, awakening black night, showing that seer a world which was only a moment ago hidden.

It's like that. The presence that entered this room through the long, intimate corridor of his wife floats across the air in the arms of a physician. He watches the child delivered into his arms, and colors, faces, names, events, the world, change.

There at the Circle

After the field went down to water. Quenched. Light on water wavering green. You met me by the water. A hand thin as. You met me by the water, a hand thin as a petal. Stranger. Where I followed no one led. Stranger. Under blue water. To touch you there. Stranger under blue water under blue sky to touch you there. I came homeless. In my youth a red chair by the window rose up and strapped me to it. A man beat me there. Under the tutelage of fists I found a quiet place and stayed. I lived in an empty field where God's light came glorious through windows into a room choked with cigarette smoke. I burrowed deep and came out on the other side, a grown man staggering to water. I met you there. Knee deep in water, a cupped handful held to your mouth. Under the blue water under the blue sky the skin fills with water the hair the skin of breasts thighs the tough hair around the dark silent center heat salt taste water there burrowing up up through the belly and out to the world to the heart around inside under blue under sky risen up risen full hurting no one in that moment hurtless.

The Passion Flower

St. Augustine on MONY Tower

"Of faith and man," the Bishop of Hippo was saying. "Of free will and the immortality of souls," he said, standing on MONY Tower, overlooking the city of Syracuse. Strand had not yet reached the roof, still climbing as he was the dense copper stairs flight after flight, but he could see St. Augustine dressed in white robes atop the black tower, his hands extended in benediction, the wind wimpling and snapping his vestments; and though the bishop spoke into the wind, Strand could hear him clearly. His voice was in fact like music.

But no meaning lingered: the words came, resolved, and disappeared, frustrating Strand, hungry not for sound but message. At the eighteenth floor on the final landing he pulled open the last door and saw before him a great black expanse. For a second. Then one wall flashed, in massive backward figures: 22°. Then darkness. Then the time: 3:57. Then darkness. And so it went as Strand peered into the clock room: temperature, darkness, time, darkness, temperature. . . .

And it will go on like this forever, Strand thought: ad infinitum.

So it had been flashing the time and temperature fifteen years ago when he first came to Syracuse, a bright student beginning graduate study in the history of religions at Syracuse University, driving a beat-up '68 Ford heading north on Route 81 from Long Island, where he had just completed a B.A. in Anthropology at Hofstra College. He was twenty-one then. He was driving without a license from his parents' house in Cold Spring Harbor. After Binghamton and a fifty-mile stretch of hills and farmland, Syracuse appeared before his eyes as a great metropolis. On his left he saw the twin towers of MONY Plaza. Though they were not the tallest buildings in the skyline—a circular Holiday Inn nearby was taller, and two or three other buildings were at least the same height—the two black towers stood out because of their proximity and symmetry; and of the two towers, the one bearing the MONY name and logo dominated because it bore also the huge digital clock and thermometer by which Syracusans checked the time and weather.

How many mornings driving up Adams on his way to campus had he checked his time against the time on MONY Tower, craning in the morning rush-hour traffic?

"Syracusans are a punctual lot," he said, watching the door to the clock room close slowly behind him. "They take time seriously in Syracuse." Then he realized that he no longer heard the saint's voice or saw his image, though now, in the clock room, he was closer to him than ever.

He turned around and it was dawn and he was returning from a business trip driving up the steep hill on Colvin Avenue after having spent the night in another city with another woman. He was on his way home and it was snowing slightly and the studded snows on his late-model car ripped up the ice and snow on the ground and carried him easily up the hill. It was a magnificent dawn: it had snowed hard all night and the snow had cleansed everything. It weighed heavily on the trees, bending the branches. Snow and ice hanging from rooftops made the dawn bright and comforting, and Strand was warm in the driver's seat when he made a sharp right-hand turn into his driveway. But the driveway had not been shoveled and the car faltered on the incline, the spinning of the rear wheels making a whistling noise that sizzled along the street. Strand cursed his boy John for not having shoveled the drive, and his wife for not having made him. The boy will be fifteen soon, he thought, and should learn to accept responsibility.

He got out of the car and left it running. He could feel the arctic cold air in his mouth and nose and eyes as he walked up the driveway to the garage for a snow shovel. The snow squeaked under his shoes. And there was his son John sitting up behind the juniper bush, frozen. Strand looked at him for a long time. The boy was sitting up straight, his legs extended along the ground, his torso forming a right angle to his legs. His skin was bluish white and covered with a light dusting of snow. A string of fluid was frozen in a thick line from his shirt collar to the corner of his mouth, where it distorted the shape of his upper lip. His eyes were closed. Strand touched him and the body was frozen to the ground. It didn't move.

Strand heard a great noise in the clock room and when he looked for the source he saw the stage at the Baths of Sozius and found himself one among hundreds in the audience. It was hot. It was August sixteen hundred years ago and Strand was both in the Baths in the past and in the clock room in the present, and St. Augustine was both on the roof in the present and at the Baths in the past, where he had just vanquished Felix in debate, as he had vanquished Fortunatus before him; and Felix had just publicly recanted the Manichean heresy, its error revealed to him by the bishop's irrefutable reason. Felix returned to the church. Fortunatus had fled. Single-handedly, through the use of pure reason, St. Augustine had defeated the heretics and thus the heresy. Strand raised his hand to ask a question. It was an important question. But he could not catch the saint's eye.

"I never intended to stay in Syracuse," he said, and though no one in the crowd responded to his statement, it was still the truth. At twenty-four, two years before completing his doctorate, Strand had married. A year later his son John was born. When he finished his education, he had a wife and a year-old son and a daughter on the way. And not a job in sight. He applied for a job with a local corporation and was hired; and that became Strand's life, though he had never planned it, could never have foreseen it, and was never happy with it. He stayed because the pay was good and he had a family to support. He settled in Syracuse and grew a potbelly.

"My boy was always restless," he said to the Christian seated alongside him, but the man's eyes were fast upon the stage where Felix was once again praising the bishop and the Church. Strand got up and walked away.

It was night and the woods felt darker and deeper than Strand remembered. All around him he could hear small life rustling through the undergrowth; above him things were moving in the trees. But before him he could see nothing but blackness. From behind he heard drums and primitive music, and he crawled on his stomach following the rhythm until he found himself at the edge of a circular clearing in the woods. In the center of the circle a campfire was burning. It was surrounded by men dressed in black robes, their heads covered with cowls.

"These are the Circumcellions," the Christian beside him whispered.

"The Circumcellions?" Strand asked.

"Heretics, fanatics, armed apostles of violence."

Strand nodded. At the edge of the circle there were amplifiers and electric guitars. On top of the amplifiers were canisters labeled Cocaine, LSD, Angel Dust, Grass, Hash, Smack, Opium, Scotch, Bourbon, Whiskey, Mescaline, and many other words that Strand did not understand.

"John," Strand asked, "do you swear this was the only time? You never tried it before and you'll never try it again?"

The boy nodded, avoiding Strand's eyes. He was staring at a wall-sized poster of a man costumed as the devil, an electric guitar slung over his shoulder, a black tear painted falling from one eye.

Strand left the room crying and returned to the darkness of MONY Tower. On the roof above him St. Augustine was preaching to the city of Syracuse, but Strand was alone in the clock room, crying. He cried until he couldn't cry any longer. Then he climbed the last flight of stairs to the roof.

The wind was blowing hard and the saint didn't seem to notice Strand as he came alongside him and looked out over the city. People were gathered everywhere, straining to hear the saint speak. Cars were parked along Route 81 for as far as Strand could see, and people were standing on their cars staring at the tower. The waters of Onondaga Lake were filled with pleasure boats filled with passengers staring at the tower. People thronged to every window and rooftop, straining to hear St. Augustine's words.

But Strand, standing beside him, couldn't hear a thing, so he sat down at the saint's feet and closed his eyes, and he fell into darkness so deep he couldn't hear the beat of his heart or the sound of the blood in his veins, and he felt he had fallen at last into a void from which there was no hope of escape.

"Tolle lege," he heard the saint whisper.

Strand opened his eyes and found himself alone in his study. Though he had heard the saint's voice, he saw no one.

"Pick up and read," the saint repeated.

Strand did not question. He picked up the book in front of him and began reading. It was a difficult text full of deep and obscure passages, but Strand read intently and when there was something he absolutely could not understand, St. Augustine whispered the meaning in his ear with a voice like light and music, until Strand felt certain he was on the road to perfect knowledge. Soon, with the help of the bishop's reason, he would understand.

It was a sweet and peaceful feeling for Strand. He felt as though he were approaching the end of his struggle, as though, alone in his study within the city of Syracuse, he had found a special place, a place within a place, a city within a city.

The Passion Flower

Who's Who In America, 1980

ESPOSITO, JOSEPH C., botanist; b. N.Y.C., Jan. 28, 1911; s. Anthony and Carmella (Caducci) E.; B.A., U. Georgia, 1932, Ph.D., U. Florida, 1937. Assoc. botanist Texas Nat. Lab., 1937–47; assoc. prof. biology U. Arizona, 1947–50; prof., head botany dept. U. Hawaii, 1950–59, dean faculty natural sci. and math., prof. botany, 1959–76; Guggenheim Found. fellow, 1949–50. Fellow AAAS (v.p. 1955); mem. AAAS, Am. Soc. Plant Physiologists, Bot. Soc. Am., Am. Soc. Devel. Biology, Fed. Am. Scientists, Phi Beta Kappa, Phi Kappa Phi. Home: 1414 Tripler Road, Sunset Beach, Hawaii, 96712. *The things of this world seem incredibly delicate to me, and the most delicate thing among them is the flower. I have dedicated my life to botany. If I had it all to do over again, I wouldn't, and probably couldn't, change a thing.*

Brooklyn, '18

Asunta brought it home, carrying it with an air of reverence, as if she were holding in her hands something mystical and delicate. She hung it a few feet from the window, in a walk-in closet, from a hot water pipe, black and sweat-covered. It needed, she said, the steam and the heat, and she pointed, in the harsh light from a bulb hanging by a wire from the ceiling, at the ten petals of the flower, saying they were the ten faithful apostles: *See these, they're the apostles that followed Our Lord and never betrayed or denied him.* And at the styles and stamens: *These the three nails and these the hammers that they used when they crucified Jesus.* Touching delicately, first, each of the anthers: *These mean the five wounds Our Lord suffered;* then running a sharp pointed and scarlet nail around the outer corona: *These, the crown of thorns He was made to wear.*

Brooklyn

I remember it only as a jungle of concrete and stone; summer nights with families on stoops; smells, like heat and excitement. The stoops of uneven texture with pebbles and small stones jutting like growths above the plane of each step; sidewalks of concrete or soft gray slate with dirt compacted in the space between the slabs. Tar or cobblestone streets. Or tar over cobblestone, with brickwork sections exposed where the tar had worn away. And two-family houses. A neighborhood of two-family houses.

I was called Monk, which was short for monkey, because I was small and wiry and ugly; and, if they chased me, I could climb a fence or a fire escape faster than any of them. Or they called me Rabbit. Playing ball with a broomstick and a Spaldene and the parked cars for bases, while I watched, sitting on a stoop or the hood of a car.

The Greenhouse

Here in Hawaii. Now. After all the long years and the silence, with what is to come only a drop in the bucket compared to what has gone before. It is lush and overgrown, rampant with species of Passifloraceae. They are my passion, my livelihood, and my hobby. In the corner, a cultivar climbs to the top of the greenhouse, its tendrils curled and knotted around a precarious construction of stakes and long handles. It is my own creation: Passiflora asunta, for my sister.

Georgia, '26

Boyhood. Fields and farmland. A million square miles of nothing, light-years from the nearest city.

After school, I'd walk home with Claire. Her skin was whiter than any I'd ever seen before or any I've seen since: cloud white, against which her lips looked crimson. She talked incessantly, her head held erect, looking directly in front of her, only occasionally glancing alongside to make sure I was still there. I listened, walking with my hands in my pockets and my eyes to the ground.

It was the last day of school; the weather intolerably hot. We walked past an empty field where May Pop grew in thick, untended clusters. She called them May Pop; her skin textured like the flower's white petals, her hair soft and blond, resting on her shoulders. Her father's car pulled up alongside us and the door swung open. She said goodbye weakly, looking straight at me.

That was the summer she moved. It was the last time I ever saw her.

Georgia, '46

I took a week off and went back for the funeral. She was buried in the same grave with my father, her name chiseled in marble beneath his name: Carmella Esposito, 1874–1946.

Someone had cleared the incarnata I planted when my father died, but you could see, in the discoloration of the gravestone, where the plant had protected it from weathering; and traces of the severed tendrils still clung to the marble. I would have planted another, but I could see that the stalks had been cut with a scythe or a mower, and I knew it would grow again on its own.

My Father

A big man and a hard worker. A carpenter and a house painter who re-laxed by working in his garden. All the years in Brooklyn, before the big job and the move to Georgia, an angry man. And explosive. He would scream at my mother. I remember his screaming.

My Brother

Almost eight years my elder, and passionately protective of his privacy. He had his own room, with an altar in the corner. On his dresser, a slender glass vase in which he kept a single white lily.

Brooklyn, '19

He had worked all summer at making an artificial pond for his garden, digging first a long shallow hole and shoveling the dirt into a wheelbarrow which I would struggle with and haul to another corner of the yard where I would spread the dirt out evenly among the bushes, raking it smooth and picking out the rocks and pebbles. All summer I worked beside him; he never encouraged; he always chided, ready to explode at my smallest error. When it was done, with its plastic lining, underground hoses, and the fountain in the center, he planted purple loosestrife and a variety of flowering plants around its edges.

He made me sit in a straight-backed chair, in the center of the kitchen, holding a crippled and broken stalk of loosestrife in his hand. He asked me calmly, *Did you trample this plant?* And when I said no, he struck me with the loosestrife, the spikes of purple flowers breaking across my cheek and temple. Over and over he asked me, and over and over I denied it. Asunta and mother in the living room crying. My brother, upstairs, at his books, studying.

The Greenhouse

I ask myself questions, swinging slowly in a wide-meshed hammock. What could I have done differently? One leg slung over the side of the hammock; my bare feet brushing the brickwork floor.

My Mother

A frail and delicate woman, who must have once been beautiful. She skittered about the house, putting things in their places, forever cleaning and arranging. Her voice shrill when speaking and shrieking when angry. She slapped me, almost always without even thinking, without even being angry—almost as a way of emphasizing what she was saying.

When I walked downstairs for breakfast, I would see her standing in front of the radiator, the rosary beads hanging from her fingers, her eyes distant and uplifted, her lips moving rapidly—a shrill, almost inaudible whining mingling with the gurgling sound of the radiator.

St. Mary's

Inside, the smallest sounds echoed. The wooden pews polished and shining; the stations of the cross, carved in marble, lining the walls. I sat in a pew in the back of the church, silently counting—fourteen genuflections, fourteen long silences; her head bowed, a dark shawl pulled over her hair, her body bent in supplication, sometimes one thin arm uplifted and grasping the marble.

As if staring at me, hanging high above the altar, with painted blood dripping from his wounds, the tormented and passionate face of Our Savior.

Brooklyn, '20

They formed a circle around me, pushing and shoving; and when I tried to break through the circle, they pushed me to the ground—in the schoolyard, with a supervisor watching and saying nothing, until one of them kicked me in the stomach and all the breath went out of me. Then he came and pushed his hands on my chest until I was breathing, and sent me into the building.

Asunta

I walked into the room without knocking and she was standing, naked, in front of the closet, a soft cloth robe dangling from her hand. Her skin looked pink and soft and smooth, but I turned and ran quickly from the room.

She found me alone in the kitchen and sat down beside me and put her arm around my shoulders and her cheek against my forehead. I was crying looking down at the floor, trying not to look at her.

She took me, first, by the hand to the sink where she filled a jar with water, then to the closet: *See how it's grown, how it's moved toward the window? These thin twisting things have curled around the dowel. They're pushing to get close to the window. It's alive. It lives on light and water. It needs us to help it survive.*

She told me first to take a drink of the water and wipe my eyes; then she picked me up by the waist and held me above her while I emptied a jar of water into the dry and dusty loam. It made a sucking and sobbing sound, like someone taking a deep breath through puckered lips.

She smelled of talcum powder from the bath; the closet smelled of mothballs and must. She said it wasn't a sin that I saw her, because I was her brother.

Dreams

Two, that recurred all through my childhood. In the first, I'm lying awake in my bed looking down the hallway to my parents' room. The door to their room is open and I can see the large wooden dresser with the hinged, three-part mirror hanging above it. There is something under the dresser. It's coming up through a hole in the floor. It grunts as it lifts the dresser on its shoulders, struggling with its weight. I try to scream, but my throat is parched and I can make only a thin, harsh, screeching sound. I watch it through darkness, trying to scream as it struggles to get out from under the dresser.

In the other, I'm standing at the bottom of a flight of stairs. At the top of the stairs, coming from behind a door just barely open, a sliver of light breaks the darkness. I mount the stairs cautiously, counting each step. I am afraid of the darkness. I am afraid of something. Still, I climb the stairs and when I reach the top, I pull open the door. Then I'm falling down the stairs, not touching the steps, more flying than falling.

I would wake up clutching at pillows, or reaching to hold the headboard, till I remembered that I was dreaming. And I'd lie awake, damp with sweat, staring out into the darkness, watching clumps of clothing take on ominous shapes, hearing strange and frightening noises.

The Greenhouse

Why do I remember some things so clearly, and forget others entirely? I remember voices, incidents, and snatches of conversations, images and pictures from the past that apparently have no meaning. Yet, I'm notorious for being forgetful.

There is a quadrangulis flourishing in the center of the room, climbing an upright dowel between the racemosa and the Innes: it bears a peculiar flower. Most people would name it Granadilla; but the filaments, which should be white and banded with purple and red, are uniformly scarlet. It's a mutation. I dreamed of it recently.

It was growing from the cracks between the tiles in my offce. It had covered the floor, walls, ceiling, door, and windows, so that I was surrounded by stalks, leaves, flowers, and tendrils—and everything was scarlet. I was sitting at my desk, calmly working on a paper, as if it were quite normal to be working in a room composed entirely of Passiflora quadrangularis. I could feel its tendrils curling between my toes and wrapped in tight strands around my ankles and calves. In the back of my mind I was thinking it was going to be difficult to get up from the desk. I'd have to spend a great deal of time cutting and hacking at the tendrils. But it didn't seem to be a matter of great concern. I continued working on my paper. Then I looked up from the desk and noticed, with only mild surprise, as if it were nothing more than a mere peculiarity, that the tendrils were not tendrils at all, but long curling whips made of leather—at their tips, an arrangement of three metal balls, and at their base, a wooden handle that grew out of the stalk. And their leaves were not leaves, but hands, severed at the wrists and surrounding the flowers: fingers, knuckles, palms and nails, all scarlet. I thought, *I must call someone; I must tell them what my work has accomplished,* and continued with my paper.

Brooklyn, '21

Asunta didn't want to come with us to Georgia. We were all seated around the table, quietly eating dinner. He allowed no talking at the table.

She began, almost in a whisper. She said *I'm in love.* We all stopped eating and looked up at her. She cleared her voice and spoke a little louder. She said she didn't want to go to Georgia. She didn't want to leave him.

At first he was quiet, listening like the rest of us, but then that hard, angry look came into his eyes and he asked her, more accusing than asking, if she was still a virgin.

She stammered, beginning to answer, but before she could speak he called her a little whore and grabbed the water pitcher and threw it across the table. She protected her face with her arm and the pitcher broke when it hit her forearm.

Her wrist was gashed and blood spilled onto the table. Through her soaked blouse I could see her skin and the outline of her bra.

I ran away from the table.

I heard him say, snarling, she was coming to Georgia.

Georgia, '32

Mother came, alone, for my graduation. I told her my first memory and she said I couldn't possibly remember, someone must have told me. (I remember struggling and screaming in a crib, kicking and flailing at the bars, with a burning in my eyes.) She said I was less than a year old: she had dropped the bars in the crib and a metal spring caught and pinched my eyelid. I swore I remembered, but she insisted I must have been told.

I asked her why they had waited so long to have me. Why so long after Anthony and Asunta. She smiled and pinched my cheeks and said You *were a gift from God.*

Brooklyn, '20

I was walking home from school, daydreaming, looking down at the pavement, so I didn't see Junior coming. When he grabbed me by the arm it was too late. I tried to run but he was older, and he pulled me into a corner, pushing me up against a stoop. I stopped struggling when he said he wasn't going to hurt me. He said he had a trick he wanted to show me. He told me to close my eyes and open my mouth.

When at first I didn't, he slapped me, knocking my head against the stoop, so I closed my eyes and opened my mouth slightly, but he told me to open it wider, so I opened it as wide as I could and he spit into the back of my throat, and I swallowed before I realized what had happened.

He was laughing like a madman in front of me, bent over and laughing hysterically.

Brooklyn, '18

She pointed at the tendrils and told me they were the whips that scourged Our Lord, and that they were incredibly delicate. That they would curl around a wisp of gossamer so light that we couldn't feel it.

And she pointed at the filaments of the outer corona and said that they stood for the rays of Christ's glory, and for the countless disciples that follow Our Savior.

And she pointed at the leaves: *See how they look like hands? Each of the five leaves are fingers. They're the clutching hands of the soldiers who persecuted Jesus.*

It had grown along and covered the whole length of the dowel, and from a thin shaft of stalk that had reached the window, a single tendril sprouted and began curling itself around the central wooden sash.

The Greenhouse

I never met a woman I wanted to settle down with and marry. I waited and waited, but it never happened. I would have liked to have children. But there was always my work, and the constant study, and the constant effort.

The flower itself is my passion: the whole plant and its environment is, of course, important, but it's the inflorescence that overwhelms me. I've thrown my life into cultivating flowers: each one has to be more beautiful than the one that precedes it.

I can't say for certain how my work became centered around Passifloraceae. Asunta, of course, has something to do with it—the special love she bore caerulea and what it stood for. And the passion flower is, I admit, a prestigious plant. The Western world's only contribution to the symbolical flowers of Christendom, it has taken its place alongside the mystical roses and Trefoils. But my love for Passifloraceae has at its heart more than my love for Asunta and more than prestige.

I believe it's the spectacular and solitary bloom that enchants me—the majesty with which it slowly unfurls, eventually dominating all the surrounding foliage, making everything around it seem small and insignificant in comparison to its beauty.

I find something wonderful in all the varied inflorescence of the passion flower's myriad species and multiple genera. And I find something in it, too, terrifying and fearful. But that, I've never been able to truly grasp or understand.

Brooklyn

Each night, at bedtime, I walked up a flight of fourteen stairs.

There was no light in the hallway, and neither was it heated, and when I told my mother that the darkness frightened me, she walked with me up the stairs, holding my hand and counting the steps as we walked.

He said I could go to bed on my own, without my mother to hold my hand.

I walked up the stairs, counting and praying, saying the name Jesus over and over, *believing* there was something lurking behind me, praying that Jesus would protect me from whatever it was I believed was hiding, crouched in the darkness.

Anthony

Not the kind of person you would expect to go into the priesthood: quiet and distant, almost sullen, he hardly ever said a word to anyone. He lived in his own world.

I woke up from a nightmare, sweating and frightened, and I heard the low sound of music coming from his room.

I knocked lightly, seeing the light under the door, but he didn't answer, so I turned the knob and entered. He was lying on his bed, with all his clothes on, staring at the ceiling, his arms crossed behind his head.

Anthony, I said. *I'm frightened.* He looked at me, not like he was angry, but more like he was looking at a stranger, as if it took him a few moments to remember who I was.

He reached up behind him and took the crucifix off the wall from above his bed and handed it to me, telling me to sleep with it under my pillow, that God would protect me.

I remember how my mother cried when he told her he was entering the priesthood.

Georgia, '32

When she first met my father, she was only a girl, fifteen years old, and he was several years older. He was a clerk in the store on the corner, and she had bought a bag full of groceries, with a lot of canned goods. When he saw that she was struggling, he jumped over the counter; and, ignoring the owner's protestations, he took the bag and walked her home.

He would come and visit her in the evening. They would sit on the stoop in front of her house. She said sometimes hours would pass when neither of them would say a word. She said no one fooled around with him. Everyone respected him. She said they were very much in love.

Brooklyn, '21

Junior held me on the ground, sitting on my waist, my arms pinned beneath his knees, while the others stood around watching and laughing. I wouldn't say that my sister was a whore, and every time I wouldn't say it, he said *Then doctor says open up wide* and shoved the Popcicle stick in my mouth while the others laughed and I struggled, squirming and twisting as he jammed the stick in my mouth, trying to pry open my teeth, and cutting and scraping my gums and the inside of my cheek. Then the stick broke in my mouth and he started slapping me, saying *Say your sister is a whore,* till I was choking and crying and at last I said it, but defiantly and fast, but he kept slapping and hitting till I said it slow and loud with everyone laughing *Asunta is a whore, Asunta is a whore.*

St. Mary's

Every Sunday, the face of Jesus staring down at me as if he were singling me out, I received communion, walking to the altar between Asunta and mother, and kneeling and waiting till the priest said something in Latin and placed the wafer on my tongue, between Asunta and mother, with the body and blood of Christ in my mouth, with his anguished face watching me from the cross hanging above the altar, watching, with God inside me.

Georgia, '25

Claire stopped talking in mid-sentence and turned and looked at me, with her eyes sparkling and mischievious, and said I *bet you can't catch me* and started running across the field. I waited a second, watching her running. Then I took off after her and caught her by the waist and fell to the ground behind her in the tall grass and weeds and May Pop growing luxuriantly in the untended field.

She dared me to kiss her, so I kissed her lightly on the lips. Then I backed away and stared at her, watching her stare at me.

She took my hand and placed it on her breast, watching my eyes, expecting me to say or do something. I felt frightened, hardly able to breathe, my breaths coming short and irregular.

I took my hand away from her breast and helped her up from the ground.

We walked the rest of the way home as if nothing had happened. She talked incessantly while I listened, my hands in my pockets, looking down at the ground.

Brooklyn, '21

It was postmarked from California. They wouldn't let me read it, but I knew it was from Asunta. I recognized the handwriting on the envelope.

He yelled at mother and told her to stop crying, and Anthony went upstairs to his room, and she went to the bathroom and closed the door, but I could still hear her sobbing.

I don't think he was even aware of my presence. He sat on the couch holding the letter in front of him, with a look in his eyes that I'd never seen before—a hurt and childish look, like a boy who'd been scolded unjustly and refused to cry.

Then he put his face in his hands, with the letter between his fingers and against his forehead, and he began to cry, his whole body shaking and his foot stamping the ground as he said something in Italian over and over, as if it were a prayer. I couldn't stop myself from running to him and putting my arms around his chest and pushing my head up against him and crying with him, saying *Please don't cry, Dad. Please don't cry.*

He put his arm around me and stroked my hair and said that Asunta was gone forever, that she had run away with a man and gone to California. He said that she was living in sin and that we would never again see her.

Then he said, *Your mother will never forgive me,* and he stood and walked upstairs to the bedroom.

Brooklyn, '21

I went, for the last time, into the closet. It was empty and dark—the clothes having already been packed and loaded, and the plant having covered the window, choking off all light.

The room smelled more than ever of must, and in the darkness I thought I could hear the plant breathing, could hear the tendrils reaching out and grabbing. I thought I could hear the plant growing.

When I heard the honking outside, I gave it water and left, closing the door behind me, and for the first few hours of the ride, long after we were gone from Brooklyn, that low sucking and sobbing sound of the plant drinking water stayed in my head as if it were music, as if it were a tune I had heard on the radio and couldn't get rid of.

The Greenhouse

This is where I feel most at home; this is my garden—it is, for me, a place of warmth and security. The thickly massed plants against the glass insure my privacy: here, I can walk as naked as Adam in Eden without fear of embarrassment. The long mesh hammock strung across the room provides a place to relax and think while I take in my surroundings. The cobblestone floor holds in the heat through the coldest of evenings— evenings when the heat pipes along the walls hiss and bang and gurgle as if they were on the edge of exploding. And the plants, in a way, provide for me—the fruit, though somewhat bitter to those unaccustomed to its taste, if properly prepared is not only edible, but delicious. The same is true of its deep-purple juices. Botany is more than it seems. It is not just pruning and trimming: it is a way of living.

I have cultivated plants and flowers of strange and evocative beauty. I think of myself as a maker of flowers, as a creator of things short-lived and magnificent. To me, every aspect of the passion flower is a constant wonder: the calyx, downed with soft brown hair; the slender, pick-like stem that supports a blade of foliage; the pistil's delicate and swaying stigma; the serrate leaf's multiple teeth edging forward in a circle; the axillary tendrils reaching and grabbing from every stalk; the scarlet petals of a flower gushing like a fountain from the throat of the calyx.

I have spent my life caring for plants and flowers, and in turn they care for me. They give me nourishment and sustenance. Most of all, they give me beauty.

Afterword

Why Short Fictions?

Over the years, I've published the work collected in this volume as poems, prose poems, short short stories, and, most recently, as short fictions. In truth, I've willingly published the work under whatever label a particular editor chose to assign it. This is not because I don't care about labels. The way you name a piece of writing influences the reader's expectations. I approached all of the work collected here, however, in the spirit of experimentation, intentionally disregarding the various conventions of form to see where such contraventions might lead. For this particular work, categories were beside the point. The earliest pieces were written after a period of intense interest in Baudelaire and Rimbaud, so when I sent them off to magazines for publication, I called them prose poems (not that this deterred editors from publishing them as stories or "sudden fiction," which was a popular term for a while). Later works were influenced by a variety of writers with various approaches to this short, prose-like form: the paragraphs published as poems by many contemporary poets, especially Robert Bly; the intensely poetic prose of W. S. Merwin; the very short stories of Ray Carver; Gertrude Stein's *Tender Buttons*; Kafka's *The Great Wall of China*; William Carlos Williams's *Kora in Hell*; the *ficciones* of Borges; the label-avoiding, very-short, story-like work of Margaret Atwood in *Murder in the Dark*; the innovative short fiction of Coover, Gass, and Barthelme; and many others, too numerous to list, including the sometimes brilliant work of less famous writers published in the nation's thriving network of literary and small press journals. Beginning in the early nineties, with the advent of personal computers and the invention of Storyspace from Eastgate Systems, I started writing hypertexts, a genre-killing kind of writing designed for the digital space of the computer screen. ("Night Water Night," is a hypertext "variant," by which I mean it is one possible reading of a piece that can, in its original hypertext form, be read in multiple sequences).

For me, all of this work has come under the personal heading of "experimental." With the publication of this collection, however, I've had to decide what to call these pieces, if for no other reason than to give librarians a hint where to shelve the book. I chose *short fictions* because, from a practical perspective, it seems like the most accurate label. *Short*, for obvious reason; and *fictions* because to call it poetry confuses everybody and because that little "s" at the end of the word *fictions* distinguishes it from the short story, with that form's traditional promise of an organic relationship between a fully realized character and significant, vividly described action. *Fictions* suggests prose making multiple promises, language, imagery, and sound patterns all foregrounded as potential ways of meaning. I'm calling the pieces collected here *short fictions* because it's a term I find essentially sensible and useful, and in the hope that the label is innocuous enough not to get in the way of the work itself.

Ed Falco
Blacksburg, Virginia